Jeremy Strong once worked in a bakery, putting the jam into three thousand doughnuts every night. Now he puts the jam in stories instead, which he finds much more exciting. At the age of three, he fell out of a first-floor bedroom window and landed on his head. His mother says that this damaged him for the rest of his life and refuses to take any responsibility. He loves writing stories because he says it is 'the only time you alone have complete control and can make anything happen'. His ambition is to make you laugh (or at least snuffle). Jeremy Strong lives near Bath with his wife, Gillie, four cats and a flying cow.

Are you feeling silly enough to read more?

**THE BATTLE FOR CHRISTMAS
THE BEAK SPEAKS
BEWARE! KILLER TOMATOES
CHICKEN SCHOOL
DINOSAUR POX
GIANT JIM AND THE HURRICANE
I'M TELLING YOU, THEY'RE ALIENS
THE INDOOR PIRATES
THE INDOOR PIRATES ON TREASURE ISLAND
INVASION OF THE CHRISTMAS PUDDINGS
THE KARATE PRINCESS
THE KARATE PRINCESS TO THE RESCUE
KRAZY COW SAVES THE WORLD – WELL, ALMOST
LET'S DO THE PHARAOH!
PANDEMONIUM AT SCHOOL
PIRATE PANDEMONIUM
THE SHOCKING ADVENTURES OF LIGHTNING LUCY
THERE'S A PHARAOH IN OUR BATH!
THERE'S A VIKING IN MY BED AND OTHER STORIES
TROUBLE WITH ANIMALS**

**Read about Streaker's adventures:
THE HUNDRED-MILE-AN-HOUR DOG
RETURN OF THE HUNDRED-MILE-AN-HOUR DOG
WANTED! THE HUNDRED-MILE-AN-HOUR DOG
LOST! THE HUNDRED-MILE-AN-HOUR DOG**

**Read about Nicholas's daft family:
MY DAD'S GOT AN ALLIGATOR!
MY GRANNY'S GREAT ESCAPE
MY MUM'S GOING TO EXPLODE!
MY BROTHER'S FAMOUS BOTTOM
MY BROTHER'S FAMOUS BOTTOM GETS PINCHED
MY BROTHER'S FAMOUS BOTTOM GOES CAMPING
MY BROTHER'S HOT CROSS BOTTOM**

**JEREMY STRONG'S LAUGH-YOUR-SOCKS-OFF
JOKE BOOK**

LAUGH YOUR SOCKS off WITH

Jeremy STRONG

The Indoor Pirates

Illustrated by

Nick Sharratt

PUFFIN

PUFFIN BOOKS

Published by the Penguin Group
Penguin Books Ltd, 80 Strand, London WC2R 0RL, England
Penguin Group (USA) Inc., 375 Hudson Street, New York, New York 10014, USA
Penguin Group (Canada), 90 Eglinton Avenue East, Suite 700, Toronto, Ontario, Canada M4P 2Y3
(a division of Pearson Penguin Canada Inc.)
Penguin Ireland, 25 St Stephen's Green, Dublin 2, Ireland (a division of Penguin Books Ltd)
Penguin Group (Australia), 250 Camberwell Road, Camberwell, Victoria 3124, Australia
(a division of Pearson Australia Group Pty Ltd)
Penguin Books India Pvt Ltd, 11 Community Centre, Panchsheel Park, New Delhi – 110 017, India
Penguin Group (NZ), 67 Apollo Drive, Rosedale, North Shore 0632, New Zealand
(a division of Pearson New Zealand Ltd)
Penguin Books (South Africa) (Pty) Ltd, 24 Sturdee Avenue, Rosebank, Johannesburg 2196, South Africa

Penguin Books Ltd, Registered Offices: 80 Strand, London WC2R 0RL, England

puffinbooks.com

First published by Dutton 1995
Published in Puffin Books 1997
This edition published 2009 for The Book People Ltd,
Hall Wood Avenue, Haydock, St Helens, WA11 9UL
1

Set in Baskerville
Made and printed in England by Clays Ltd, St Ives plc

British Library Cataloguing in Publication Data
A CIP catalogue record for this book is available from the British Library

ISBN: 978-0-141-32787-7

www.greenpenguin.co.uk

Penguin Books is committed to a sustainable future
for our business, our readers and our planet.
The book in your hands is made from paper
certified by the Forest Stewardship Council.

Contents

Introducing the Indoor Pirates

Blackpatch came from a
long line of pirates, and he
really did have a patch too
– although it was not
over one eye. It was on
the sleeve of his jacket,
where he had torn it on a
nail. His grandparents had
been pirates. His mother and
father had been pirates. It
seemed obvious that he should be a pirate
too. This was just a little unfortunate,
because Blackpatch hated the sea. In fact,
he hated water of any kind – drinking-water,
bath-water, washing-up water – and most
of all sea-water. Blackpatch wished he
didn't have to go on boats at all.

One day he got a letter from his great-grandmother, who was very ancient. She was 107, and she had patches too. There was one on her dress, one on her leather smoking-jacket (she *loved* big cigars), and another on her thumb, where she had cut it by mistake. It was quite a nasty cut, and it made Great-granny realize that she was getting too old to look after herself properly. She wanted her great-grandson to come home and see to her needs. The letter made Blackpatch very happy. At last he could live on dry land!

Off he went, and he looked after Great-granny very well until she died. (By this time she was 112.) Great-granny left her house to Blackpatch, saying that she hoped he would look after it, and the first thing that Blackpatch did was to write a letter of his own. He wrote to all his friends at sea — all the ones who didn't like it, and he asked

them to come and live with him at 25
Dolphin Street. And that was how the
Indoor Pirates began.

First of all, there was
Bald Ben. He had huge
muscles and was
immensely strong.
He could lift up
two people at once,
one under each
arm. He hadn't a
single hair on his bald
head. Instead, right in
the middle, he had a
colourful tattoo of a rose, with I LOVE
MUM written underneath. Bald Ben didn't
like going to sea because it meant missing
too much television.

Polly and Molly were twin sisters. They
looked just like each other, except that
Polly's hair was bunched out by her right

ear, and Molly's was bunched by her left
ear. They were always, ALWAYS arguing
with each other. Whatever one said, the
other said the opposite, even if it was
nonsense.

'We're sisters,' Polly might say.

'No, we're not!' Molly would snap.
'We're . . .' and she would screw up her
eyes desperately '. . . brothers!'

'You're stupid,' Polly would answer.

'You're the one that's stupid,' Molly
would counter, and so it would go on. The

twins didn't like going to sea because they couldn't swim.

The fifth and last Indoor Pirate was Lumpy Lawson. He didn't look lumpy at all – in fact, he was tall and rather skinny with it, despite his love of food. No matter how much he ate, he never got any fatter. Lumpy Lawson did all the cooking (and most of the shopping too) and whenever he made porridge, there were gigantic stodgy lumps in it and that was how he got his name. He didn't like going on boats because if he tried to make soup at sea, it always slopped over the top of the pan. The boiling soup splattered on to his feet and made him leap about shouting very, VERY bad words like 'Jigglepops!' and 'Pumplespizz!'

Of course, it was no good having five pirates without a leader, and Captain Blackpatch decided that there was only one possible choice – namely himself. This was because:

1 It was his house.
2 He said so.
3 He could shout louder than anyone else.
4 He liked bossing people about and,
5 See 2.

Blackpatch's first decision was to make himself Captain. Then he made Lumpy Lawson the Ship's Cook, Bald Ben his First Mate, and told the twins he would make them walk the gangplank if they didn't stop quarrelling straight away.

The Indoor Pirates did not want anyone to know where they lived, so they took the number off the front door and hung a skull-and-crossbones flag from the chimney-pot instead. All the neighbours knew immediately that they had pirates living near them, but they didn't mind, because the pirates stayed indoors most of the time. (That was how they got their name.)

Old Mrs Bishop, who lived next door, even cut flowers from her garden every so often and gave them to Bald Ben, because

she thought he was rather sweet. Besides, the pirates were not very good at their job.

First of all, since they didn't like the sea, they didn't have a boat. (They had several small boats that they played with in the bath, but they didn't have a proper, full-size pirate boat with an anchor and lots of sails and cannons and ropes.)

They were very fond of their little house, even if it was a bit cramped inside. It only had three bedrooms. The Captain had swiped the biggest – what a surprise! – and that left the twins sharing bunk-beds in one, and Bald Ben and Lumpy Lawson in the other. (Ben had a hammock. He liked to rock himself to sleep.)

The Indoor Pirates liked to think of their house as a ship, even though they weren't at sea, so they had taken out all the stairs and replaced them with rope rigging. Then they had painted all the walls blue with

little white, fluffy clouds
and hung big plastic sea-
gulls from the ceilings.

They worried about
being attacked by other
pirates, so beside each
window they always kept a
good range of weapons:
catapults, swords and
several large buckets of
dishwater. (The pirates all

thought that soaking an enemy with water was THE WORST POSSIBLE THING that they could do to them.)

The Indoor Pirates were very happy at 25 Dolphin Street. For a couple of months everything went swimmingly (even though the twins didn't like swimming), but trouble was never far away.

1 A Visit from the Postman

One morning Captain Blackpatch was standing in the front room, surrounded by heaps of clothes. He was very busy doing the ironing. Normally the Captain was very good at avoiding the ironing (not to mention the cooking, cleaning, dusting, washing, vacuuming and gardening), but now he was hot, cross and fed up.

He reckoned he had been ironing for at least two hours and there was still a pile as big as an armchair. He slammed the

iron down on the table, where it made a
big black burn mark and a nasty smell.
'This is ridiculous!' he bellowed. 'Pirates
shouldn't have to do ironing. We should
have slaves to do our work for us.'

'That's a good idea,' said Polly.

'No, it isn't,' Molly immediately butted
in. 'It's a *really* good idea.'

'That's more or less what I said,' Polly
shouted.

'Isn't.'

'Is.'

'Isn't.'

'Is.'

'SHUT UP!' roared Captain Blackpatch.
'I have worked out a brilliant plan. We all
hide behind the front door and wait for
someone to call. When they knock on the
door, we leap out and grab them, drag
them inside and keep them prisoner.
Then,' and here the Captain took a deep

breath before he proudly announced the next bit, 'we say to them: "You are our slave and you have to do everything we say or we'll be very nasty to you!" And they will be so scared that they'll do anything – especially the ironing.'

The Indoor Pirates all agreed that this was an excellent plan and they went and crouched down behind the front door. They made quite a heap, all squashed up together. Bald Ben seemed worried and at last he piped up,

'We don't really have to be nasty to them, do we?'

'We're pirates,' grumbled Captain Blackpatch. 'We're supposed to be nasty.'

'I know, I know, but can't we just *say* we're nasty, and not actually *be* nasty?'

Blackpatch heaved a sigh, but before he could answer he was interrupted by the twins quarrelling.

'Stop pushing,' complained Molly.

'I'm not pushing, I'm pulling,' said Polly.

'Stop pulling, then!'

'I'm not. I'm pushing now!'

'Sssh!' said Lumpy, peering through the letter-box. 'Someone is coming up the path.'

The letter-box banged in Lumpy's long face and a letter was stuffed into his mouth, much to his surprise. Captain Blackpatch ignored Lumpy's muffled squeaks and shouted. 'All aboard! Get him!'

The Indoor Pirates leaped up, instantly

fell over each other and sat down again in
such a muddled heap that heads were stuck
between legs, arms appeared to come out
of ears, and the whole lot looked like a
major wrestling disaster. The front door
slowly swung open and the postman stared
down at a wriggling pile of pirates, one of

whom had a letter sticking out of his
mouth.

The postman was so astonished that he
just stood there. This gave the pirates
plenty of time to stagger to their feet. Bald
Ben reached out with two brawny arms,
picked up the postman and marched into
the house. The postman was plonked down
on a chair in the back room and the
Indoor Pirates crowded round, glaring
fiercely at their victim. Lumpy Lawson
poked his face right up close to the
postman's and bared his teeth
threateningly. (He'd taken out the letter.)
'We are your slaves and we will do
anything you say!' he hissed.

'No, we're not!' shouted Polly.

'Yes, we are!' cried Molly.

'No, we're not, stupid. We're not *his*
slaves. He's *our* slave.'

Captain Blackpatch was hopping from

one foot to the other. 'Jumping jellyfish! Let me do it,' he roared. 'Listen to me, postie-person. You are our slave and you have to do everything we say. Right?' The postman blinked back at them. He took off his spectacles and began to polish them on his shirt.

'I'm very sorry,' he began, 'but I can't be your slave today because I already have a job as a postman.'

This unexpected reply completely threw the Indoor Pirates, except for Bald Ben, who seemed quite relieved. 'Does that mean we don't have to be nasty to you?' he asked.

'Oh yes, definitely,' nodded the postman, carefully putting his glasses back on. 'I wouldn't recommend any nastiness at all.'

Bald Ben was very pleased to hear this, but Lumpy suddenly gave a howl of horror. He turned deathly white and held out the letter that the postman had just delivered. Lumpy handed it over to Captain Blackpatch, who stared at it, glared at it and then had to sit down in an armchair to get over the shock.

'Whatever is it?' whispered the twins.

'It's the electricity bill,' announced the Captain, just as if he was telling them that the Earth had exploded and everyone was dead. 'Unless we pay up in four weeks, we are going to be cut off.'

'Cut off?' repeated Bald Ben, scratching his tattooed head. 'What does that mean?'

'It means they cut off your legs,' said Polly.

'No,' said Molly, 'it means they cut off your arms.'

'*And* your legs,' insisted Polly. 'And head. And nose. And ears and hair and . . .'

'Excuse me,' said the postman. 'It means that the electricity company will stop supplying the house with electricity unless you pay the bill. If they cut you off, you won't have any lights. You won't be able to cook or watch television or anything.'

'That is just what I was going to say,' growled the Captain. 'How much money has everyone got?'

The Indoor Pirates turned out their pockets and made a pile on the table. Altogether they had one paper-clip, three elastic bands, a lot of fluff, a broken penknife, a very crumpled, signed portrait of Captain Hook and a small heap of coins.

Captain Blackpatch scowled at the pile. 'That's not nearly enough. We need ten times that. Where on earth are we going to find the money?' He stared at the other pirates, and they stared back at him with wild, blank faces.

'THINK!' roared the Captain. 'Think hard!' A deep silence fell on the room. The five pirates paced round and round with strange, twisted expressions on their faces, which showed just how hard they were thinking. At last Blackpatch gave a triumphant shout.

'I've got it! We hold the postman here to ransom! We keep him prisoner and we send a note to the Post Office saying that they must pay us . . . a million pounds, or they will never get their postman back.'

'That's brilliant!' cried Lumpy. 'We shall be rich!'

Even Bald Ben, who was beginning to think that the postman was quite a nice chap, thought it was a good idea. Captain Blackpatch sat down at the table and carefully wrote a ransom demand.

Deer Post Offisss
We hav got your postman.
Giv us a millyon ponds
or you wont get him bak
EVER !!!
Singed: The Indoor Pirates
Bald Ben xxx Captin Blackpatch
Lumxpy Lawsoxn
Molly ⟶ Polly
Me not her! ⟵ Me not her!

'Now, all we have to do is send this letter to the Post Office,' chuckled Captain Blackpatch. 'Soon we shall be as rich as kings!'

The postman got to his feet and smiled at everyone. 'As it happens, I was just on my way to the Post Office. I'll take the letter with me if you like.'

Captain Blackpatch was overcome. 'You are kind. What a jolly nice postman you are. Thank you so much. You will deliver it safely, won't you?'

'Of course,' said the postman. 'That's my job.' He took the ransom demand, let himself out by the front door and walked off down the road, whistling cheerfully.

The Indoor Pirates watched him go and then hurried into the front room, where they sat down by the window so that they could see when the postman was coming back with the million pounds.

While they waited, Lumpy Lawson made everyone a lumpy cup of tea. (He left the teabags in the cups.) They drank their tea and they waited. Lunch-time came and went. Tea-time came and went. At last Captain Blackpatch got to his feet.

'I think that postman must have got lost,' he muttered.

'Some horrible men might have kidnapped him!' suggested Bald Ben angrily.

'What are we going to do about the electricity bill?' moaned Lumpy. 'If I can't use the fridge, half our food will go mouldy.'

Captain Blackpatch started to climb the rope rigging up to his Captain's quarters. 'I can't think any more today,' he grunted. 'I've already had two clever ideas in one day and now I'm worn out. I expect I shall have another clever idea when I wake up tomorrow morning. Obviously nobody else is going to think of anything useful.' He scowled down at his crew. 'I'm going to bed. Batten down the hatches. Good-night!'

'Good-night,' said Molly.

'Good-morning!' said Polly.

2 The Treasure Ship

There was a great deal of clattering on
Dolphin Street. The refuse truck was
slowly making its way down the road. The
dustmen were collecting rubbish from
every house and throwing it into the back
of the truck. The Indoor Pirates had two
sacks of rubbish and Polly carried them to
the back of the truck. 'There's a lot of stuff
in there!' she said. 'I never knew there was
so much rubbish.'

Fred mopped his florid face with a big spotty handkerchief. 'It's amazing what some people throw out,' he said, shaking his head in disbelief. 'This truck is like a treasure chest some weeks.' Polly's eyes almost fell out of their sockets. She tried to appear as calm as possible.

'Oh?' she squeaked. 'Treasure, you say?'

'Every week,' nodded Fred, stuffing his handkerchief inside his baseball cap before shoving it back on his head. 'We get old tellys, foodmixers — all sorts of things that can still be used. We always get lots of tools.'

Just as Fred said 'tools', his mate Tony gave a huge sneeze and drowned his words, but Polly was quite certain that Fred had said 'we always get lots of *jewels*'. She didn't bother to stop and listen to any more. Polly was already half-way up the garden path before Fred had finished counting on his stubby fingers all the treasures: 'old spades, saws, hammers, screwdrivers . . .'

Polly almost smashed the front door off its hinges, she was so excited. She clawed her way up the rigging and barged into the Captain's quarters, where Captain Blackpatch was having breakfast in bed. (Blackpatch had breakfast in bed every Thursday. And also every Tuesday. And also Sundays, Fridays, Mondays, Wednesdays and Saturdays.)

Polly blurted out everything about the refuse truck full of treasure. Blackpatch was rather puzzled at first. He wondered why a rubbish truck should be used for carrying jewels.

'Don't you see?' cried Polly. 'It's a trick! Nobody would ever think of looking in the back of a dustcart for jewels!' Of course, it had to be a trick! Blackpatch grinned from one big ear to the other. Those dustmen were fiendishly clever – fancy hiding jewels in the rubbish!

At this, even Captain Blackpatch got so excited that he spread honey on the back of his teddy. He yelled for the rest of the crew and they came hurrying in. 'Good work, Polly,' said the Captain. 'Prancing prawns, we're going to be rich, lads! We shall be able to pay our electricity bill for the next thousand years!'

'But how are we going to get the

treasure?' asked Bald Ben, hoping very much that it would not involve hitting anybody.

Captain Blackpatch leaped out of bed, even though he wasn't wearing any pyjamas. (He'd gone to sleep in his clothes as usual.) He fixed his crew with a fierce grin. 'We shall wait until the treasure ship sails down our street and then we'll have a boarding party.'

'Hurrah – a boarding party!' shouted Lumpy. 'It's ages since we had a party. I'll make the cakes. I'll do some of those nice chocolatey ones with white icing on the top, and some butterfly-sponges with hundreds and thousands to make them look pretty. I'll bake lots of mini sausage-rolls and put little cubes of cheese on sticks and . . .'

'It's not that kind of party, you dopey doughnut,' roared Captain Blackpatch. 'A boarding party is when we get our swords and we all hang on ropes and go swinging across to the enemy ship and jump on her and take her over and get all the treasure. That's what a boarding party is.'

Lumpy Lawson was crestfallen. 'No cakes or sausage-rolls?' he asked. The other pirates sadly shook their heads. They quite fancied the kind of party Lumpy had just described. However, at least they would get the treasure.

'I'm going to be rich!' said Polly, rubbing her hands.

'No, you're not,' snapped Molly. '*I'm* going to be rich!'

'That's what I said, I'm going to be rich,' Polly repeated.

'No, that's what *I* said. *I'm* going to be rich,' insisted Molly.

'SHUT UP!' bellowed Captain Blackpatch. 'Everybody get your sword. We've got a week before the treasure-ship dustcart-thingummy comes back and we need all the practice we can get so that we are perfect on the day.'

The Indoor Pirates fetched their swords and they practised swinging on ropes and getting into very noisy and dangerous sword fights. They always used wooden swords.

Some while back, they'd had proper metal ones which they tucked into their belts, but every time they pulled out their swords they sliced through their belts and their trousers fell down. Captain Blackpatch decided that wooden swords were a lot better.

They practised day after day. The only

time they stopped was when Bald Ben
discovered his teddy was missing. There
was a dreadful fuss and he just would not
be comforted. Captain Blackpatch offered
Ben his own teddy, although it still had a
rather sticky bottom.

'I don't want your teddy, I want mine,'
wailed Ben. 'I've had him for years and
years and he is my very best friend.'

'Do stop blubbing,' pleaded Molly. 'You
can have my toothbrush that's like a
dinosaur.'

'No, you can have *my* dinosaur

toothbrush,' Polly promised. 'It's bigger and better than hers.'

It was no use. Bald Ben wanted his teddy and that was the one thing that could not be found. They searched the house from top to bottom, from side to side, and then front to back. Ben did not stop wailing until it was bin-day once more and the Indoor Pirates were getting ready to steal all the jewels from the refuse truck.

Molly put out two sacks of rubbish next to the trees on either side of the road. The pirates grabbed their swords and clambered up into the leafy branches. 'Wait for my signal,' whispered Blackpatch, his eyes glinting from between the leaves. The pirates grasped their ropes.

'Can we have chocolate sponge *after* this?' mumbled Lumpy Lawson.

'If we get the treasure,' hissed the Captain, 'you can have a chocolate sponge as big as a ship. Listen – they're coming!'

With a great clanking and grinding, the refuse truck clattered to a halt between the two trees. Down jumped Fred and Tony to

collect the sacks. They were startled by a
loud yell from the middle of a tree.

'Boarding party – let's get 'em!' And
with swords firmly gripped between their

teeth, the Indoor Pirates swung into action.

Lumpy Lawson forgot to hold his rope and crashed to the ground. 'Oh, fuzzyfigs!'

Bald Ben went zooming straight into the side of the truck, which made his eyes spin round and round as if they were on a spin-cycle.

Molly and Polly landed on the roof of the truck and started to fight each other before they remembered they were on the same side.

Captain Blackpatch swung down beside the driver's cab and dangled at the open window. He glared savagely at Dave the driver. 'Hurfisheruk! Giffusherezzer!'

Dave looked back at the fierce bearded face. 'Beg your pardon?'

'Hurfisheruk! Giffusherezzer!' bellowed Blackpatch.

Dave rested his hairy arms on the steering-wheel. 'If you take that sword out

of your mouth I might be able to hear
what you are saying,' he suggested calmly.
The Captain, who was still holding the
rope with both hands, struggled to spit out
the sword.

'Splurrrgh! This is our truck!' he snarled.
'Give us the treasure!'

'What treasure?' asked Dave. 'We
haven't got any treasure. All we've got is
rubbish.'

'Ha!' cried Blackpatch. 'I knew you'd say
that! You think I'm stupid, don't you?'

'Yes,' nodded Dave. 'And you are, too.'
Fred and Tony nudged each other and
grinned.

'You can't fool me,' growled the Captain.
'If you don't give us the treasure, I'll cut off
your arms and you'll be swimming in pools
of your own blood.'

'No, we won't,' said Dave. 'If you cut off
our arms, we won't be able to swim at all.'

'DON'T ARGUE!' thundered Captain
Blackpatch. 'We have boarded your ship
and taken it over. Now, we want the jewels,
and you are going to unload them into our
front garden. GET ON WITH IT!'

The dustmen looked at each other and
shrugged. Tony tugged his cap further
down his weaselly face. 'I always did think
these pirates were a bit daft,' he muttered.

'Better do as they say,' said Fred. 'The
customer is always right.'

Dave frowned at the Captain's sword.
The tip was almost sticking into his nose.
'Stop poking me and I'll back up to your
garden,' he said. The engine hummed and
hurred. The rear of the truck lifted higher
and higher until with a sudden *whoosh!*
out spilled all the rubbish. Within a few
minutes the garden was piled high with a
stinking, messy mountain of muck.

'Help yourselves!' shouted Dave, as Tony

and Fred climbed into the cab alongside
him and they all went off for an early tea-
break.

'Wonderful!' cried Polly.

'It's more than one-derful,' argued Molly.
'It's two-derful.'

'Two-derful?' said Polly. 'What's two-
derful?'

'One more than one-derful, of course,'
Molly answered. 'Two-derful. If it was even

more wonderful it might be three-derful, or even six-derful.'

'You're the most stupid human being in the whole world,' muttered Polly, and she turned back to the stink-pile. The excited pirates pulled out sacks and emptied them. They plunged their arms deep among old fish bones, smelly socks, mouldy cheese wrappers, squidgy tomatoes, soggy pizzas, and hunted for jewels.

'Anyone found anything?' rasped Captain Blackpatch, trying to brush away several thousand flies that seemed to find him very attractive.

'I've got an old hammer,' said Lumpy Lawson.

'I've found a saw,' said Molly.

'I saw the saw first,' Polly began.

'No! I saw the saw you saw first. You saw my saw.'

'QUIET!' boomed the captain. He

straightened his aching back. 'It's no good.
Those dustmen must have suspected us
right from the start. They've hidden the
jewels somewhere else. This is just a filthy
pile of rubbish. There's
nothing here at all.'

'Oh yes there is!' cried
Bald Ben triumphantly.
'Look what I've found
– my teddy! He was
right at the bottom
of the pile!' Ben wiped

a big smear of baked beans from his chin
and his face split into a huge grin. He was
happy at last.

Next door, a window
was flung open and Mrs
Bishop leaned out.
'Captain Blackpatch,' she
said accusingly, 'I do hope
you are not going to leave
that horrible smelly mess
there all week?' And she

glared at the pirates with stern eyes.
Blackpatch gritted his teeth.

'We wouldn't dream of it, Mrs Bishop.
The crew are just about to bag it all up
again.' And while the crew bagged all the
rubbish once more, Blackpatch went inside
and bagged the bathroom.

He ran a deep bath and got in with all
his clothes on. After all, they were just as
dirty as he was. He lay there for an hour,

grumbling and growling to himself, and
wondering how they would ever manage to
pay that electricity bill. The little plastic
boat he had been bombarding with small
bits of soap finally sank and Captain
Blackpatch closed his eyes. Outside the
bathroom, four very smelly pirates
patiently waited their turn for a bath.

'You stink,' said Molly.

'*You* stink!' said Polly.

Bald Ben sniffed a couple of
times. 'I think we all stink,'
he observed ruefully, and
they stood and listened
to the loud snores
coming from the
other side of
the bathroom
door.

3 The Hunt Goes On

Lumpy Lawson was the first to see the notice. He had gone to the shops and was busily using up what little money they had left to buy important supplies – eggs, bacon, chocolate, cereals, chocolate, crisps, fruit, biscuits (chocolate ones), milk and chocolate. And there, in the supermarket window, was the notice.

GRAND EASTER TREASURE HUNT

COME TO THE PARK ON SATURDAY!

EVERYONE WELCOME

Lumpy almost dropped the shopping in his haste to get back to 25 Dolphin Street.

He ran all the way there, so by the time he arrived he could barely speak for panting.

'We're going-a-huff-a-huff-a-huff . . .'

Captain Blackpatch, who was busily supervising the housework by lying in an armchair with both eyes closed, opened one fierce eye and glowered at the ship's cook. 'What? What did you say?'

'We're going to be-a-huff-a-huff-a-huff . . .'

'Shivering sharks!' shouted the captain. 'Get a grip on yourself!'

'I'll grip him, Captain,' offered Bald Ben, wrapping his massively muscled arms around Lumpy's body and lifting him completely clear of the ground. Lumpy's arms and legs thrashed about wildly as he tried to breathe. The Captain was beside himself.

'I didn't mean that kind of grip, you big, bald barnacle! Look – he's turning purple.

Let him go at once.'

'Oh – sorry, Captain.' Ben obediently let go.

Lumpy fell to the floor and so did the shopping. There was a loud crash and a large milky puddle appeared beside

Lumpy, quickly joined by some ready-scrambled eggs. Lumpy struggled to his feet. 'We're going to be rich! Everything is going to be all right. There's a Treasure Hunt in the park on Saturday!' And he told the pirates about the poster in the supermarket window.

'Saturday,' said Molly. 'That's tomorrow.'

'No, it isn't,' argued Polly. 'It's the day after today.'

'The day after today *is* tomorrow!'

'It isn't,' insisted Polly. 'The day after today is the day before the day after the day after tomorrow.'

Molly was still trying to puzzle that one out when Captain Blackpatch interrupted. 'We've only got four days left, lads, and then the electricity company are going to cut us off. We've got to get our hands on that treasure in the park tomorrow.'

'What kind of treasure do you think it

might be?' asked Molly. The Captain tugged at his stormy beard.

'Gold, I expect, and silver too. Maybe some pearl necklaces and diamond rings. But we could have a fight on our hands. Suppose there are other pirates there? The notice says everyone is welcome. What we need is a plan, and who makes the best plans around here?'

The four other pirates looked at each other, perplexed. Who did make the best plans? They hadn't got a clue. Captain Blackpatch tore at his hair.

'I do, you huge hairy half-wits! Now, let me sit in this nice comfy armchair so that I can have a proper think.' And he drove the pirates from the front room with a kick of one slippered foot.

Lumpy Lawson went stomping back to the shops to buy some more milk and eggs. (He got some chocolate too.) Bald Ben knitted a little cardigan for his teddy bear. Molly and Polly went upstairs to their bunk-beds and had a flaming row that ended with each sister throwing the other's entire bedding out of the window. This came as a bit of a surprise to old Mrs Bishop, who later discovered Polly's pillow and Molly's night-dress draped over one of her beautiful rose-bushes.

The following morning, Lumpy made everyone a lumpy picnic to take with them.

(He made sardine sandwiches with whole sardines.) The pirates grabbed their swords and set off for the park.

'Here we are, lads,' hissed Captain Blackpatch. 'Keep an eye out for pirates.'

The park was certainly full of people, although there didn't seem to be any other pirates. There were a great number of children and a few parents too, but the Indoor Pirates hardly noticed the crowds. They had spotted something so wonderful

that all they could do was fix their eyes on it and sigh deeply.

It was a climbing-frame. It was big, and it was painted bright red and bright green. As if that wasn't enough, the climbing-frame had been built in the shape of a pirate galleon.

'Now, *that's* the kind of ship I like,' said Captain Blackpatch. 'One that's anchored in concrete. Come on, let's seize her!'

The pirates drew their swords and rushed across the play area, yelling and snarling and driving the children from the climbing-frame. The children hurried off to find the park-keeper so that they could complain, while the Indoor Pirates swarmed over their captured prize.

'This is the best ship we've ever had,' grinned Polly.

'It isn't,' said Molly. 'I went on a ship twice as big as this.'

'Well, I went on a ship three times bigger,' Polly butted in.

'My ship had a thousand cannons!' cried Molly.

'My ship had a million cannons,' shouted Polly, 'and its masts reached the sky and its sails were as big as clouds and it could go as fast as a hurricane . . .' she panted. Molly stared back at her sister.

'Well, my ship was even bigger,' she said simply. 'So there.'

Polly drew her sword and was threatening a fight to the death, but Captain Blackpatch had had enough and he ordered her up to the top of the mast to act as look-out, and a good thing too. Hardly had Polly taken up position when she gave a cry of alarm. 'Pirate on the starboard bow, Captain!' she cried.

Sure enough, a large, red-faced park-keeper with big boots and bristling

moustache was marching straight towards
them, surrounded by an excited gaggle of
children. 'Look here,' he complained. 'You
big pirates can't play here. This is for
children.'

'I like your hat,' said Lumpy Lawson
admiringly. 'Can I have it?'

'Of course not. This hat is the property
of the Parks and Gardens Department.'
The park-keeper wagged a large and
menacing finger at the pirates. 'Now, get
off at once!'

There was no way that the Indoor
Pirates were going to have their newly won
ship taken away from them. Captain
Blackpatch whispered something in Bald
Ben's ear.

'Raaargh!' snarled Ben, suddenly leaping
overboard. The children screamed and
scattered like frightened shrimps, while Ben
seized the surprised park-keeper, tucked
him under his arm and returned to the
ship.

'Well done!' whooped
Captain Blackpatch.
'Our first prisoner. Tie
him to the gangplank
over there!' And he
jabbed a finger
towards the slide.
Bald Ben carried
the struggling park-keeper to the top of the
slide and tied him firmly to the railings.

(Lumpy Lawson had whipped his hat and was proudly wearing it.) The poor park-keeper shouted at the children, pleading to be rescued, but the children had better things to do. The Great Treasure Hunt had started.

All over the park excited children were rushing about, finding Easter eggs. They were hidden under bushes. They were taped to tree branches, and the children gathered them from their hiding-places, clutching the shiny foil-wrapped eggs in their arms. Polly gave another excited yell.

'I spy treasure!' she cried, her round eyes fixed on the shiny eggs. 'I spy huge jewels and masses of them!'

The Indoor Pirates were astonished. Never had they seen such wonderful rubies and sapphires and emeralds! 'Ha! We're going to be rich after all!' yelled Blackpatch, drawing his sword. 'Raiding party – follow me!'

Round the park went the pirates, poking and prodding with their swords and gathering jewels wherever they went. The children ran off crying and the pirates ran off with their arms bulging with booty. They went back to the ship and piled up their treasures. They sat round the heap and picked up the jewels one by one.

'My ruby is worth a trillion pounds,'
sighed Polly.

'My emerald is worth more than the
Bank of England,' Molly claimed.

'And mine is worth more than all the
banks in the world,' said Polly.

Molly glanced mischievously at her sister.
'Mine is worth the most,' she said, 'because
I've got yours!' Molly made a sudden grab
for Polly's ruby egg. 'Oh!' they both cried,
as the jewel crumbled into little pieces.
Bits of chocolate tumbled out from the split
foil wrapper.

For a few moments, the pirates stared at

the broken jewel, then all at once they began scrummaging through their treasures. 'They're all the same!' roared Captain Blackpatch. 'We've been diddled. These aren't jewels – they're chocolate eggs!'

Lumpy Lawson stuck a piece in his mouth and sucked on it happily. 'Oh well, it could be worse,' he pointed out, and he was right, because at that very moment a tidal wave of furious children swept over them.

The robbed children had gone off to find the park-keeper again and when they found him tied to the top of the slide, they quickly released him. Now they were on the war-path. Fifty-seven children, a large, red (hat-less) park-keeper, three dogs and a pony (which had run away from giving pony rides) rushed up and threw themselves upon the pirates.

'Give us back our eggs!'

'Down with the pirates!'

It was the biggest, noisiest, biff-and-bammiest fight that the park had ever seen, and the pirates got by far the worst of it.

'Ouch!' (That was Bald Ben.)

'Eeeek!' (That was Polly.)

'I said Eeeek first!' (That was Molly.)

'Bumbleflip!' (That was Lumpy Lawson.)

Dust and grass flew everywhere. Arms whirled round, mostly with fists on them. Legs scrabbled in the dirt. Easter

eggs came whizzing out from the middle of this human hurricane, and so did several lumpy sardine sandwiches and a park-keeper's hat, much to everyone's surprise.

At last, all the heaving and wriggling and shouting stopped. The children gathered up their rather battered eggs and marched away happily. The park-keeper went off to try and get all the dents out of his hat, and that just left the Indoor Pirates, somewhere inside an enormous cloud of dust.

The dust slowly settled and there they were, all tied up in one big heap. 'I want to go home,' sniffed Ben. Captain Blackpatch was wondering why it had got dark so early. (Someone had rammed his hat down over his eyes.)

They sat there for a very long time, until at last the Captain realized that nobody was going to come and untie them. After several efforts, they managed to stand up. They set off for home, waddling up the road like some weird ten-legged beastie from the bottom of the sea. Blackpatch couldn't see where he was going.

'This way!' cried Polly.

'THIS way!' yelled Molly.

'Stop tugging!'

'I'm not tugging, I'm clugging,' said Molly.

'There's no such thing as clugging!'

'Yes, there is. It's what you do when

you're not tugging.' Molly gave such a tug
against her sister that all five of them fell
over and began rolling across the grass.

'This is ridiculous!' roared Captain
Blackpatch. 'What's going on? Where are
we? I've just about had enough of you

twins! Splurrgh!' He spat a large clump of grass from his mouth and the pirates rolled merrily on. It was a miracle that they got back home at all.

4 A Few House Alterations

The twins were arguing AGAIN, busily hitting each other with their pillows. 'You always have the top bunk,' snarled Polly.

'No, I don't!' shouted Molly, giving her sister such a slosh round the head that her

pillow burst and the room was filled with tiny white feathers. 'You've had the top bunk all this week.'

'And you had it all last month!' Polly cried.

'Well, you had it all last year – and the year before that and the year before that and the year before that . . .'

'You had it last all century!' screamed Polly, trying to smother her sister's face with her pillow. 'You had it before we were even born!'

'Stop – STOP!' thundered the Captain, 'before I make you both walk the plank. I won't have any more of this. I can't bear it any longer.'

Bald Ben waved a thick hairy arm in the air. (Luckily it

was his.) 'I've got a good idea.' The other pirates stopped in their tracks and stared at him. Bald Ben had an idea? Ben never had ideas. Ben was kind, Ben was strong and Ben was helpful – but he didn't have ideas.

Ben grinned back at the others. 'Why don't we take the bunk-beds apart? We could put one bed on each side of the bedroom and then there won't be any bunks to argue about.'

Captain Blackpatch was impressed. 'You're a clever lad, Ben, have one of my fruit gums. Take a yellow one, I don't like them.'

Everybody went upstairs and watched while Ben did all the lifting himself, even though it made his face look like boiled beetroot. The beds were separated and put on either side of the little room.

'There,' said the Captain. 'Let's see you quarrel about that.'

Polly threw herself triumphantly on one of the beds. 'This is mine!' she cried, daring Molly to say that it wasn't. Molly smiled sweetly and sauntered across to the other bed.

'This is mine,' she agreed, and the Indoor Pirates smiled with relief. 'Because it's better than Polly's bed and it's the best bed in the whole world!'

Polly was on her feet in an instant, eyes blazing. 'Mine's the best bed in the galaxy – no, in the universe!' Blackpatch almost exploded. His eyes became narrow, furious slits. His mouth turned into such a snarl that all his teeth could be seen, glinting like daggers. He drew his sword and was advancing menacingly on the twins, when Bald Ben waved his hairy arm again.

'I've had another idea!' he shouted. The pirates groaned. This was almost becoming a habit. 'Let's put one of the beds downstairs, then Polly and Molly won't be able to see each other at night.'

'Excellent idea, Ben,' said Captain Blackpatch. 'Have another yellow fruit gum.'

Unfortunately, try as they might, the Indoor Pirates could not get Polly's bed out through the door. They even tried the window, but that was unsuccessful too. Eventually they gave up and the Captain stomped off in a huff, complaining that the real problem was that their house was too small. 'Three bedrooms aren't enough,' he grumbled.

'You've got a room all of your own,' said

Lumpy peevishly. 'We all have to share. You're the only one with a room of your own.'

Captain Blackpatch turned very red and quickly changed the subject. 'We are about to have our electricity cut off. Do you understand how serious that is? What we need is treasure. If we had treasure we could pay our electricity bill and . . .' Blackpatch grinned craftily. 'We could buy a bigger house, with five bedrooms.'

The other pirates liked the sound of this new house, but treasure was difficult to find. It wasn't the sort of thing that was just left lying around, and that was why Lumpy Lawson was so surprised when he discovered a treasure map in the kitchen cupboard. He had been looking for something useful, like chocolate biscuits, when he found the map stuck to the bottom of the marmalade jar.

(Actually, it wasn't a map at all. Long before the Indoor Pirates had moved into Number 25, Great-granny Blackpatch had needed a new front gate. She had written down the measurements on a scrap of paper: 75 centimetres wide, 90 centimetres high and 5 centimetres deep.)

'Look – a treasure map!' shouted Lumpy, and he carefully spread the map on the

kitchen table. The other pirates wrinkled their noses and wondered what it all meant.

Captain Blackpatch tugged hard at his beard, his eyebrows knitting together in a fierce frown. 'It's directions,' he growled. 'It means start at the gate.' The pirates crowded round excitedly. A real treasure map! Their eyes grew shiny and their mouths fell open, which was a little unfortunate because Bald Ben began to dribble. (He nearly always dribbled when he thought about gold and jewels and coins.)

'What's 75 W?' asked Polly.

'Don't you know?' Molly sneered.

'Tell us, then,' Polly dared her sister.

'It means . . . woodlice!' cried Molly, saying the first thing she could think of that began with a 'w'.

'Seventy-five woodlice!' snarled Captain

Blackpatch. 'What kind of treasure is that?
It's W for West. That's what it means.
75 West.'

'What about 90 h?' asked Ben.

'It's not an 'h', it's an 'n' for North.
90 North,' said Captain Blackpatch, 'and
then it's 5 down. Start at the gate, 75 paces
West, 90 paces North and dig down 5 paces.
Come on – let's go!'

The pirates took the instructions for a
front gate, grabbed some spades and
shovels and rushed out to the front garden.
'This way!' cried Blackpatch, consulting his
compass. The pirates tramped across the
garden, climbed in through their own
window and marched West across the front
room. Then they went North through to
the kitchen, still counting, into the back
garden, over the wall and into Mrs
Bishop's beautiful garden next door.

'88, 89, 90!' cried the Captain, standing

in the middle of a rather splendid flower-bed. 'Start digging.'

Plants and mud and garden gnomes began flying everywhere. The hole got deeper and deeper and Mrs Bishop's flowers flew higher and higher as the pirates dug up every single one. 'Anybody found anything?' asked the Captain impatiently.

'I've got some worms,' said Molly.

'I've got more worms than you,' Polly muttered.

'I've got an old shoe,' cried Bald Ben.

'Oh, it's mine!'

'I've got backache,' grumbled Lumpy.

At that moment, a terrible scream came from the house and Mrs Bishop came rushing out on her walking-frame as fast as she could manage. 'Aargh! What are you doing to my wonderful garden? You stupid, stupid pirates! Get out at once!' She was so angry she seized her walking-frame and hurled it at the rapidly retreating pirates.

'Ouch!' cried Bald Ben as it bounced off his bottom.

The pirates scrambled back over the wall, rushed inside, locked the back-door and pulled the curtains. 'Phew,' sighed Lumpy. 'That was a narrow escape.'

'Not for me it wasn't,' muttered Ben, rubbing his rear. The Captain was re-examining the crumpled map.

'I don't think we counted right,' he said, 'It can't mean paces. It must mean feet. Come on, back to the gate.'

The pirates tramped outside and started again, even though it was beginning to get dark. The Captain carefully counted every step. '88, 89, 90. Now, dig.' The Indoor Pirates eyed their great leader.

'But, Captain, we're in the middle of our own back room.'

'So is the treasure then!' cried Blackpatch. 'Dig!'

They set to right away. Out of the window went the furniture. Up came the carpet and the floor-boards. The pirates began digging and very shortly there was a deep hole and an ever-increasing pile of rubble all round the edge.

'I've hit something!' cried Lumpy
Lawson. 'Look!'

Captain Blackpatch scrambled down
into the hole and brushed dirt away from
the object, until he revealed a large, black,
metal box. A breathless silence filled the
small room. 'Look, lads,' whispered the
Captain, his eyes shining
like diamonds. 'It's the
treasure. We've found
the treasure. Our
troubles are over!
Hand me that
pickaxe, Molly,
and let's see
what's in
store for us!'

Blackpatch seized the pickaxe, raised it
high above his head and brought it
smashing down on the big black treasure
chest.

What an explosion! Enormous crackling sparks sizzled and spat from the box. The Indoor Pirates were hurled into the air, where they bounced off the ceiling before crashing back down into the hole, one on top of the other. Bricks and plaster, dust and floor-boards and shreds of carpet roared around the room in a violent whirlwind, clattering and battering at the poor pirates.

Great cracks shot up the walls and went zigzagging across the ceiling. They splintered in every direction, split open and widened. Then, just as the pirates were thinking that the world had come to an end, a great, gaping hole opened in the ceiling and Polly's bed fell through and landed on their heads.

'OW!' yelled all five at once, before collapsing back at the bottom of the smoking pit.

All along Dolphin Street the neighbours came rushing out of their houses to see why all their lights, all the street lights and half the town's lights had suddenly gone out. They looked across at Number 25.

The windows had burst from their frames. The front door was hanging on one hinge. The chimney-pot (along with a very tattered skull-and-crossbones) had been hurled high into the sky before smashing into smithereens on the road below. Tiles slid slowly down the roof, sliced through the air and then crashed into the gardens, front and back.

Deep inside Number 25 the big black box smouldered, and black, choking smoke poured from the broken casing. Molly poked it with a grimy foot. 'That's not a treasure chest,' she coughed angrily. 'That was an electricity junction box and we've just cut off our own electricity.'

'Yes, it is, and we have,' nodded Polly and the twins stared in horror at each other. They had actually agreed on something!

Bald Ben sniffed loudly. 'I don't like it when it's dark,' he moaned. 'It's scary and I've got a nasty bang on my head where Polly's bed fell on me and a bruise on my bottom and there's something sharp sticking in my back and I'm probably going to die.'

Lumpy Lawson crawled across to his friend. 'Lean forward so that I can see,' he said, peering at Ben's back. 'It's all right – you're not going to die. You were lying on

this old tin.' Lumpy pulled a small,
battered tin from the rubble. As he did, the
lid fell off and out tumbled a thick wad of
paper with an elastic band round it.

'Money!' screamed Captain Blackpatch,
seizing the wad and breaking the band.
'Money! Money! Money!' He threw the
hundred-pound notes into the air and they
rained gently down upon the soot-covered
pirates. 'Great-granny must have hidden
this away years ago! We're rich, lads! We

can pay the electricity bill and repair all
this damage, and buy . . .'

'. . . an enormous chocolate sponge-cake?'
suggested Lumpy hopefully.

'Definitely an enormous chocolate
sponge-cake,' agreed the Captain.

Bald Ben began to giggle. 'Look, we've
even got Polly's bed downstairs.' And he
pointed at the rather dented bed that was
lying on its side. Polly put it the right way
up and stretched out on it. 'I'm sleeping
downstairs tonight,' she said wearily.

'And I'm sleeping upstairs,' yawned
Molly, both of them too exhausted to argue
any longer.

Captain Blackpatch rested back against a
pile of rubble and gave a deeply satisfied
sigh. He picked up a few hundred-pound
notes. 'Money at last,' he murmured. 'And
do you know, I think we have found
something even better to treasure.'

The Indoor Pirates looked at their
leader. What was he talking about?
Blackpatch grinned at them through the

dusty gloom of the exploded room. 'Listen – what can you hear? Nothing. That is the sound of silence. Molly and Polly have stopped quarrelling. Now that really *is* something to treasure!'

14½ Things You Didn't Know About

Jeremy Strong

* * * * * * * * * * * * * * * * * * *

1. He loves eating liquorice.

2. He used to like diving. He once dived from the high board and his trunks came off!

3. He used to play electric violin in a rock band called **THE INEDIBLE CHEESE SANDWICH**.

4. He got a 100-metre swimming certificate when he couldn't even swim.

5. When he was five, he sat on a heater and burnt his bottom.

6. Jeremy used to look after a dog that kept eating his underpants. (No – **NOT** while he was wearing them!)

7. When he was five, he left a basin tap running with the plug in and flooded the bathroom.

8. He can make his ears waggle.

9. He has visited over a thousand schools.

10. He once scored minus ten in an exam! That's ten less than nothing!

11. His hair has gone grey, but his mind hasn't.

12. He'd like to have a pet tiger.

13. He'd like to learn the piano.

14. He has dreadful handwriting.

And a half . . . His favourite hobby is sleeping. He's very good at it.

Ask Jeremy

Of all the books you have written, which one is your favourite?

I loved writing both **KRAZY KOW SAVES THE WORLD – WELL, ALMOST** and **STUFF**, my first book for teenagers. Both these made me laugh out loud while I was writing and I was pleased with the overall result in each case. I also love writing the stories about Nicholas and his daft family – **MY DAD**, **MY MUM**, **MY BROTHER** and so on.

If you couldn't be a writer what would you be?

Well, I'd be pretty fed up for a start, because writing was the one thing I knew I wanted to do from the age of nine onward. But if I DID have to do something else, I would love to be either an accomplished pianist or an artist of some sort. Music and art have played a big part in my whole life and I would love to be involved in them in some way.

What's the best thing about writing stories?

Oh dear – so many things to say here! Getting paid for making things up is pretty high on the list! It's also something you do on your own, inside your own head – nobody can interfere with that. The only boss you have is yourself. And you are creating something that nobody else has made before you. I also love making my readers laugh and want to read more and more.

**Did you ever have a nightmare teacher?
(And who was your best ever?)**

My nightmare at primary school was Mrs Chappell, long since dead. I knew her secret – she was not actually human. She was a Tyrannosaurus rex in disguise. She taught me for two years when I was in Y5 and Y6, and we didn't like each other at all. My best ever was when I was in Y3 and Y4. Her name was Miss Cox, and she was the one who first encouraged me to write stories. She was brilliant. Sadly, she is long dead too.

When you were a kid you used to play kiss-chase. Did you always do the chasing or did anyone ever chase you?!

I usually did the chasing, but when I got chased, I didn't bother to run very fast! Maybe I shouldn't admit to that! We didn't play kiss-chase at school – it was usually played during holidays. If we had tried playing it at school we would have been in serious trouble. Mind you, I seemed to spend most of my time in trouble of one sort or another, so maybe it wouldn't have mattered that much.